THE LITTLE BOOK OF
DRAG

THE LITTLE BOOK OF

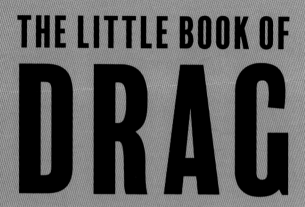

DRAG

Divas, drag family, drama, and deliciousness

BRANDI AMARA SKYY

DOG 'n' BONE

DEDICATION

For all those who have ever wanted to do drag, and for all those who told them they couldn't.

To my family, both blood and chosen, for always being there when I needed to buff up my shine.

And to my wife for teaching me that the only queen I ever needed to be was me, untucked.

Published in 2022 by
Dog 'n' Bone Books
An imprint of Ryland Peters &
Small Ltd

20–21 Jockey's Fields,
London WC1R 4BW

341 E 116th St, New York,
NY 10029

www.rylandpeters.com

10 9 8 7 6 5 4 3 2 1

Text, design, and illustration ©
Dog 'n' Bone Books 2022

A CIP catalog record for this book is available from the Library of Congress and the British Library.

ISBN: 978-1-912983-53-7

Printed in China

Designer: Geoff Borin
Illustrator: Camila Gray

Art director: Sally Powell
Creative director: Leslie Harrington
Head of production: Patricia Harrington
Publishing manager: Penny Craig
Publisher: Cindy Richards

Contents

INTRODUCTION

Divas, Kings, and Royal in-betweens to the dance floor Please!

and yes...

THAT MEANS *YOU TOO!*

Because if you are reading this, I bet my bottom lashes that you are just as flawlessly fabulous as any drag royalty I know!

So stop everything you're doing (except reading this book!) and get your dancing shoes ready because you are about to embark on the most fabulously flawless journey— not to mention the grandest time *Of. Your. LIFE!*

Your road to all things deliciously drag starts now! So let's start with what brought you here ready to sashay down the wonderland of drag? Maybe you're reading the opening pages of this book because...

- **You love the cover.** (*Me too!*)

- **You LOOOOOVE all things drag and want to learn more about it.** (*That was me 20+ years ago.*)

- *You are uber-intrigued about all the current drag hype and you are secretly—or overtly—dying to know more.* #tellmeallthethings

Or maybe this isn't your first time at the drag rodeo? Maybe you're a lot like me and you're here because…

- **You are an avid and longtime supporter of the art form of drag.**

- **You never miss a local drag show.**

- **You are a drag queen/king/artist, or an aspiring one!**

Whatever grand design brought you to this book, you're here because drag, like something shiny in your favorite store, has caught your attention and you're excited to learn more.

And that, hunties, is exactly what we are going to do! Wherever along the rainbow, gender, or drag spectrum you find your flawless self on, **welcome to this wonderful, delicious, and divine world of drag!**

All are welcomed here!

If this is your first venture into Dragland, I know you have tooooons of questions. Questions like… Who are you? What exactly is this thing we call drag? Where did it come from? Why is it important?

*A*nd we are going to kiki about **AAAALL** of them! As you continue reading, you'll soon discover that the only thing "little" about this book is its size and title. Because from here on out, you're going to get **BIG**, **DIVERSE**, **DELICIOUS** answers to all these questions and more!

But before we go galavanting all around town in our most extravagant coiffed wig, allow me to introduce you to your very own tricked-out drag guide—me! Or as my favorite (and original) female drag queen, Miss Piggy, would say, *moi!*

I'm Brandi, and after seeing my first drag queen, Aaron Davis, at 16, I knew that out of all the worlds that existed this world of glamour, genderplay, performance, and rhinestones was the one I was meant to live in. No other expression of femininity—or what I call in my first book flamboyant femininity which is a queer-based femininity (*aka* flamininity)—spoke to my queer heart quite like Aaron Davis' 6-inch stilettos, mile-hile hair, and back handsprings. I spent my entire twenties and thirties performing, competing, writing, living, and experiencing drag from the inside out.

In my adventures in Dragland, there were queens, crowns, pageants, travels, tears, and titles galore.

There were also many firsts, including being crowned the first Miss USofA Diva in 2014 and writing the first book centered on female drag queens. But what all those experiences helped me uncover was a truth about drag that I would spend the rest of my life sharing and advocating on behalf of—drag as a queer culture art form. A way in which many of us in the community discover ourselves. Drag taught me more about myself as a humxn, artist, and soul than just about anything else.

I love drag so, so much. And I owe a lot of my strength, perseverance, and attitude—a queen is nothing without a little glam-a-tude ;)—to drag.

So when I was asked to write this book, I set my intention to write the **BEST** little book about drag that this world has ever seen, as a tribute and yet another love letter to an art form that has given our community—and now others—so, so much.

Thank you, drag!

And here's the real tea: in all my decades of research, I haven't found a book quite like the one you're about to embark on now. A book that includes and examines drag from a multi-dimensional, diverse, and all-encompassing perspective, lens, and love. One that speaks to the diverse subcultures of drag and loves all of them, equally.

There's a lot of heart in this book. My own and the beats of those dragsters who have come before me—and all the ones that will come after. It's a little book with a **BIG ASS** heart. And as I've said in my previous books, if we—the live-rs, the experience-rs of said history—don't write our own story, record our own history, someone outside of us will. Saying yes to writing this book is my contribution to us writing our own history.

The only way to really know drag and to record its nuances—as well as its **GRANDIOSITY**—is to have lived it.

May this book help you live out your own drag dreams—or find them!

Now let's get fearless in our adventures, hunties!

Terminology

is a drag

One of the things I've always loved about drag is its language. Here you will find a quick but fierce alphabetical guide to some of the most popular drag styles and lingo.

Bake or **baking** is used to describe the time we allow for our foundation and highlighter to set into our drag mug, *aka* bake.

Charity Queens/Kings/Artists Those folxs who only drag for charity purposes and on the charity circuit.

Drag Artist An all-inclusive and gender-neutral term to refer to all dragsters who prefer not to gender-label their art. (And my term of choice).

Drag King An AFAB (assigned female at birth), cis-woman, or transman who drags as male. As far as popularity is concerned, drag kings are a far-away second to the drag queen. A new wave of femme kings is emerging that blurs the gender lines even more—and I am so here for it!

Drag Queen An AMAB (assigned male at birth), cis-man, or transwoman who drags as a female. The most popular and mainstream of all the drag artists. Drag queen can also be a generic term for all drag artists—like how some people use Coke to describe all sodas including Dr. Pepper, Pepsi, etc.

Female Drag Queen An all-inclusive umbrella term for cis-women or AFAB women who do drag. Other terms include AFAB Queen, Diva, Femme Queen, Bio Queen, Lady Queen, and Faux Queen.

Female Impersonator Same as above. However, their drag specialty is the impersonation of a particular singer, star, or celebrity. Female impersonation, as in impersonating a female in style, manner, and dress, was also one of drag's first and main definitions.

Kiki I've use this word throughout the book and it means a cute little get-together and talk with your favorite friends!

Look Queen/King/Artist A drag artist who may not necessarily perform, but serves up a sickening drag look anyway. A drag artist who serves serious mug and face.

Male Impersonator or Entertainer This term is used to describe a cis or AMAB male who also drags as male. Like the faux queen, he could also be called a faux king. A good example of this form of drag is what we see in the Mr. Gay USofA pageant system.

Sickening When something is just too dope to handle. The person, place, or thing is just so extra and extravagant that it's reached the level of sickening!

Sisters of Perpetual Indulgence Also a charity and activist-based "order of queer and drag nuns." [1]

Slay the kids I also use this phrase throughout the book and it means to bring the audience, people, crowd to their knees (actually more like to the floor) with our fierceness.

Deliciousness

WHAT IS DRAG?

*A*lright, friends. You've seen the shows. You feel like you've got the fundamentals of reading down. And you're pretty sure that if you ever decided to lip-sync for your life you'd come out the winner. You've got "Drag Race" knowledge for days, but have you ever stopped to ask yourself what drag is? What is this art form made mainstream by RuPaul that we all love so much? Where did it begin? And who were the first drag artists?

In this first deliciously divine section, we're going to take a peek behind the curtain of drag and dig our heels into the many definitions, identities, and styles of drag. The beauty of drag is in the power of its diversity and that power comes from the people that perform it and their experiences.

But before we dive into all the goods, we would be tragically remiss if we didn't begin our adventures without first kiki-ing a bit about gender. Some might argue that there is no drag without gender. Others might say that gender has nothing to do with it. Both are right—and wrong. The real tea is that in order for drag to make sense, we've gotta first understand why gender is so important in drag.

So what is gender?

While a complete deep dive into this question is beyond the scope of this little book, how we answer this question—collectively, socially, and individually—plays a huge role in how we define drag. Because drag, despite all its nuance and complexities, is the queering, blurring, and erasure of gender. Drag is one way that we, the LGBTQIA+ community, have deconstructed, subverted,

Agender

Nonbinary

Lesbian

Trans

Bisexual

Genderqueer

Intersex

and reconstructed gender. And because drag has been rooted in gender norms and patriarchal systems, it is super-important for us to have a common understanding and collective definition (at least for the duration that you're reading this book) of what gender is. So for the sake of our drag adventures together, let's use the following definition of gender as we move throughout this book:

"Gender is a social construct that is deeply rooted in our collective consciousness and therefore a hard systemic habit to break."

Keeping this definition of gender in mind as we move through the vastness of this subject will help us really understand why drag was and is so important to us and subversive to the mainstream. Now, let's get on with the show!

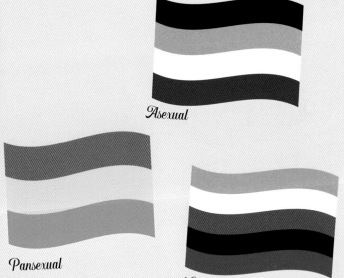

Asexual

Pansexual

Genderfluid

Delectable definitions

When I saw my first drag queen at 16, I had no idea, intellectually, what I was watching. But my body, my heart, my intuition knew it was something unlike anything I had seen or experienced before. I knew there was something radically special about what I was witnessing: a glamazon in a rhinestone-encrusted bodysuit, hair coiffed to the gods, doing back handsprings in those 6-inch stilettos.

There's something magical about drag queens that I have yet to put my finger on. Maybe it's the hyper-representation of imagination, creativity, possibility, and blurring of so many lines including gender. Or maybe it's that we can see a little bit of ourselves reflected in their art—the self that we wish we could be. The fierce, bold, and flawlessly epic one that gives no f***s, stacks their lashes for filth, and knows how to put on a good show.

The realiTEA of drag is that it is as much as about becoming someone or something as it is about owning, releasing, shining, and sharing all the pieces of you to be seen. To be felt. To be expressed. To be experienced.

Because drag is an experience—both for the audience and performer. From the audience's perspective, drag is a glamorous world of heels, stashes, lashes, and tons of fabulousness and what appears to be make-believe.

To those who perform it—especially our queer gente—drag is a vehicle of queer expression. What kind of expression? Everything from self-expression to identity expression (and exploration) to joy, love, creativity, sex.

One of the reasons we tune into "RuPaul's Drag Race" or "Dragula" every week is to see how each of the drag artists interprets the weekly challenge and infuses it with their own creativity and personal expression. The creative interpretation, reflected in the drag artists' costumes, music choices, and performance, is really what the art of drag is all about. This no-holds-barred, offbeat creativity is often referred to as camp.

Drag artists will often take something traditional, say a movie like *Dracula* and "camp it up"—meaning they will

queer it up by making it (and being) super-extra in the expression of it. Some great examples of camp are drag names like Hedda Lettuce, and Sarah Palegic (a cis-gender lady queen who is also paraplegic), and the drag kings in our Drag Profile at the end of this chapter. Camp is a big element and emphasis of drag. And its campy aspects lead us down a road of gaiety and joy when it comes to defining drag.

Drag is *fun*

Drag is *camp*

Drag is *for everyone*

But drag is also deeply personal to those whose lives were and are profiled and criminalized because of it.

In the twentieth century—particularly the 1940s, '50s, and '60s—drag, called cross-dressing at the time, was effectively outlawed. Prior to Stonewall, police arrested LGBTQIA+ folxs for not wearing "three articles of gender-appropriate clothing." This benchmark for the minimum amount of gender-appropriate dress that could protect you from arrest (commonly assumed to be law) was drawn from the masquerade laws, which originally had nothing to do with drag or cross-dressing. However, it was still used by the police to enforce the criminalization of homosexuality and the meaning of wearing too much of the opposite gender's clothing.

And so drag became an outright act of rebellion, protest, and subversion—even after the Stonewall Riots. (Check out the Scare, Terrorist, and Genderf**k styles of drag on pages 48–51 for more on this.) And there are those who would like to see both PRIDE and drag return to their socio-political activist and protest roots—or at least bring more awareness to them.

But, for a lot of the LGBTQIA+ community, drag is also about gender exploration. Many drag artists begin performing drag because they love it, only to find that through their performances they've unraveled and revealed (to themselves) their own gender identity. In this instance, drag can also be a means to acquiring self-knowledge and understanding.

Because of this history of persecution of queer folxs who have performed it…

Drag is *rebellion*

Drag is *queer expression*

Drag is *a revolution*

It is all these things and more. But that's what makes drag such a beautiful, radical, and ever-evolving art form: it's a living art that is a prismatic reflection of its people, and there are so many more elements and variables to what drag is than I can fit in here.

So what is drag?

I believe the most important thing to remember as we continue down our drag adventures is that drag is so much more than what we see on TV. It's complex, has radical and activist roots (as well as some misogynistic ones—more on that in the next chapter), and is deeply nuanced—just like the folxs who perform it.

The point is that when we say we love drag, we have to mean that we love ALL sides of drag. We can love it for all the feels it gives us, and the fierceness that it provokes within us, but we also have to honor and respect the complexity from which the art form evolved. And since we're friends, let's get a bit more real: we cannot claim to be lovers of drag if we don't love, know, and respect all versions, experiences, elements, and the people in it. We owe it to drag to see and celebrate it in all its glory.

So now that we have a more multidimensional idea of all the many things that drag is, let's have a quick kiki about some of the ways that we define drag.

In 2009, RuPaul debuted his campy definition of drag with the acronym of C.U.N.T. which stands for Charisma, Uniqueness, Nerve, and Talent. This definition has become one of his many catchphrases on the show. But even RuPaul's kitschy definition is based upon the most traditional, popular, and accepted way to define drag which goes something a little like this:

Drag is *a performance of gender opposites.*

Let's take RuPaul for example. RuPaul was assigned male at birth (AMAB), he identifies as male, but he performs as a female—his perceived gender "opposite." Same for assigned female at birth (AFAB) drag king performers like Landon Cider. Landon was assigned female at birth, identifies as female, and thus, under this gender opposite definition of drag, performs as male.

But defining drag as a performance of gender opposites poses some real problems—especially in our current state of hyper gender awareness and deconstruction of traditional gender binaries. This definition is actively being used—even by RuPaul himself—to police drag's borders by drawing clear, straight lines between what is drag and what isn't. And we all know, there's nothing straight about us—or our drag!

Even so, this way of defining drag is still the most pervasive. We can chalk that up to history (more on that in the next chapter) but we can also see how the popularity of "RuPaul's Drag Race" and more specifically RuPaul's binary view of drag further perpetuates this gender opposite definition as the "only" and "right" one. And this notion of "rightness" is often used as "proof" as to why AFAB/AMAB or cis-identifying women and men can't do drag because they aren't performing as their gender opposite.

We non-traditional drag artists—and many modern-day drag artists—are here to tell you that this definition is antiquated, tired, old, and in need of a queer-over. And isn't that what we were

FIERCE *Drag* FACT

This performance of gender opposite is known as gender subversion—the turning of traditional notions, beliefs, and socially accepted gender norms on its head. Judith Butler wrote extensively about gender performative theory and the subversion of gender in their book *Gender Trouble* (see page 139.)

born to do? I believe that we can respect and pay homage to drag roots while still having space for drag to evolve and grow. And this growing space (and pains) are what we as a culture and community are experiencing now with the heated back and forth battles online of whether or not AFAB/cis-gender women "can do drag."

Perhaps most important of all is that *drag is a living art*. *Drag is queer creative expression*. And because drag is ever-evolving and changing, those who perform it and are in the thick of it are the ones who often get to define it. History only takes us so far. The future of everything, drag included, is up to us.

And guess what? Drag will continue to grow and as it does it will become an even more radically inclusive art form than it is—even now. Our role, as artists, performers, and lovers of drag, is to let our drag flag fly high—in whatever hue of diversity it decides to take!

Drag Styles

So what about all those delicious folxs who perform drag? What are the many ways in which they describe and identify their art form? Just like there are many definitions of drag, there are many ways that performers choose to identify their art. We're going to take a look at some of the most popular ones now, but before we do, let's take a hot second to make an important differentiation before proceeding down the identity lane.

In this section, we're talking about how someone chooses to identify their art versus how they choose to identify their gender. These are two different things that may or may not intersect, collide, or align. So when we say drag queen, king, look queen, etc., we are commenting on the person's performance and/or artistic identity, not their gender identity.

It's also important to note that how each drag artist chooses to identify their art is usually directly reflective of how they define drag. Traditional drag queens will call their art female impersonation or drag queening. If an AFAB queen sees drag as pure camp, then they will

willingly embrace the kitschy identity of "faux queen"—
many of my San Francisco drag sisters fall into this camp
(*get it!*). If they see drag as an outlet to embrace all things
glamorous and fabulous about themselves, then their
drag expression will be glam and/or pageantry drag and
their artistic identity will align with those beliefs too. If
they see drag as an artistic outlet and queer expression
(as I do) then they will most often allow themselves to
dance between all styles and identify under the term
"drag artist."

Make sense?

As with all things in this book, we proceed with caution.
Caution because not all these identities will be agreed
upon—no one book, person, or artist will ever get it all
right for everyone. Caution that as our definitions and
expression of drag continue to grow, push, and evolve,
a whole new lexicon within drag and those who perform
it begins to evolve. Caution because although I have
deeply tried, neither this—nor any other list—is meant to
(or can) be an all-inclusive list. Humxn expression is way
too diverse to ever be captured in any list completely.

And caution because there are TONS of drag artists who choose not to define themselves in a particular way—and that is beautifully valid too. This section isn't meant to feed into the fragmentation of our artistic endeavors as much as its intention is to present what is ultimately a complex, highly personalized expression of art in the clearest and most deliciously digestible way. But what I do know for sure is that we can all agree that we are a fantabulous community that has created its own language and lexicon to reflect how beautifully diverse and amazing our art of drag is! #allthefeels

Now click your heels together, friends of Dorothy (and Toto too!) and get ready to follow the rainbow brick road to the wonderful land of drag styles and identities.

Drag Queen

Divine. RuPaul. Aurora Sexton. Tommie Ross. Dame Edna Everage (pictured above). The Boulet Brothers. Jenna Skyy. Asia O'Hara. Alyssa Edwards. Lawanda Jackson. Kim Chi. These are just some of the MANY queens in the game. Drag queens have historically been defined as AMAB (assigned male at birth) men who perform in "female" garb. And while we'll kiki more in the next chapter about the history of drag, drag queens have traditionally performed as female.

While shows like "RuPaul's Drag Race" adhere to this traditional definition of drag, many transgender women perform drag, and like their AFAB counterparts, are demanding to be included in the narrative.

More than any other subsection of drag, we know all about our drag queens. That's because most mainstream drag shows, commercials, and appearances focus solely on this style of drag without contextualizing drag as the diverse performance that it is. Even today, the queen is seen as synonymous with drag in general whereas the drag king and other drag artists have to work that much harder to see the same kind of career, social, and cultural advancement.

Drag King

Wang Newton. Mo B. Dick. Ivory Onyx. Landon Cider. Phantom. Tenderoni. Miles Long. Gage Gatlyn. All drag kings. Like their queen counterparts, drag kings run the gamut of the gender spectrum from AFAB to cis-women to transmen. Drag kings will typically perform a variety of masculinity on stage—including femme and flamboyant masculinity.

With the emergence of pageants like Dragula and Alaska's Drag Queen of the Year which are all-inclusive to female drag queens and drag kings, we're seeing drag kings rise, slowly, into mainstream drag narratives. Drag kings have just as rich a history and legacy as queens (more on that in the next chapter.)

FIERCE *Drag* FACT

Landon Cider was the first drag king to win a national-based and televised drag pageant— "Dragula" season 3. Tenderoni was the first drag king to win Alaska's *Drag Queen of the Year* pageant.

Female Drag Queen

Fauxnique. Ruby Scott. Holestar. Sigourney Beaver. Bea Dazzler. Sascha Macias. Myself. Are all female drag queens. We were AFAB (assigned female at birth) and while we may not necessarily identify our drag that way it's a commonality between us.

Female drag queen is an umbrella term used for all AFAB and cis-female forms of drag. Other popular female drag queen identifiers include faux queen, bio queen, AFAB queen, diva, femme queen, lady queen, and each queen has their own reasons for choosing the identifier they do.

For me at the start of my career faux queen felt good because it was kitschy, fun, and born from our queer campiness and the 1996 San Francisco Faux Queen Pageant. It didn't carry the loadedness it does now. Eventually, I organically shifted to drag queen, then female drag queen, and finally to drag artist—which is the identifier I currently claim.

Drag Artist

While this identifier is relatively new and definitely more of a slow burn than the others, I define it as performers who want to de-center gender from their drag and just let their art speak for itself.

Drag artist can also be used as an umbrella term for all drag forms. As we continue on our adventures in drag, I will be using the term "drag artist" when speaking about drag in general. Identifiers such as queen, king, faux, AFAB, etc. will only be used when referring directly to specific artists and when explaining their respective functions.

Delish Styles

There are about as many different styles of drag as there is diversity of folxs who perform it. To better illustrate the wide-ranging scope of drag, I've included a shortlist of some of the many other expressions it can take. Some are more traditional, most are still evolving. Please note that this is not an exhaustive list but is shared in the hope of giving all of us a deeper understanding of how personal (and radical) drag can be, has been, and will continue to be.

Impersonation (female or male)

This style is when the drag artist impersonates another artist, celebrity, performer, or sometimes even other drag queens. Some impersonations include famous singers like Lady Gaga, Prince, David Bowie, Liza Minnelli (see opposite), other celebrities like RuPaul, Tim McGraw, and even cartoon characters like Jessica Rabbit and Lumiere from *Beauty and the Beast*. I've also seen male entertainers (*aka* male drag kings or faux kings) don RuPaul boy drag!

Typically the performer will take great care in replicating the costume to the T. For example, one of my favorite queens, Aurora Sexton, does a sickeningly good impersonation of Miss Piggy. It's drag! It's camp! It's pure creative female impersonation. Or using myself as an example, in my 2013 bid for Miss Oklahoma Diva USofA the pageant theme was Hollywood and I impersonated J. Lo's iconic green Versace red carpet moment by carefully recreating the dress. The same is true for all kinds of celebrity impersonations like Madonna with her cone bra and signature blonde ponytail and movie and TV roles such as Dorothy from *The Wizard of Oz* or Delta Burke from *Designing Women*.

Ball drag

While this style was made popular with the general public by Jennie Livingston's 1990 thesis documentary, *Paris is Burning*, and brought to new modern audiences with Ryan Murphy's 2018–2021 show, "Pose," this queer form of expression has a deep history and lineage in the Black queer and trans community. More than a style of drag, this community and pageant-walk style drag was born in the late 1800s from Black queer folxs' need to carve out safe spaces for themselves.

Ball culture rose to prominence during the Harlem Renaissance and is still HUGE today (see page 140 for a piece I wrote about Dallas' local Ball scene). This variety of drag includes signature walks, battles, and all-night shows where folxs compete in a variety of categories.

Pageant (or glam) drag

This style of drag focuses on all things glamour and standardized feminine—think heels, ball gowns, big hair, and long nails and lashes. Pageant drag often mimics red carpet events like the Met Gala or cis-female beauty pageants like Miss USA and Miss Universe.

Typically, this style of drag is what's expected in the gown portion of a drag pageant. This is a complete head-to-toe look, with the gown tying into the hairstyle, the jewelry, and the shoes. Pageant drag is the most glamazonian out of all the drag styles and the style that we see the most in mainstream media.

A great example of this style is anytime RuPaul hits the runway and sashays down the catwalk before introducing the constestants' challenge on his show.

Scare drag

This style of drag started in the 1960s as a form of protest against the "three gender-appropriate articles of clothing" convention, which we'll talk about more in the next chapter. This style of drag was intended to confuse mainstream society about the gender of the drag artist. They create confusion by marrying the clothes of both genders to create a new, hodgepodge androgynous gender and style.

Scare drag is often seen as a softer version of Terrorist and/or Genderf**k drag. Scare drag is thought to be a little more haphazardly thought out, intentionalized, and pieced together than Terrorist and Genderf**k drag.

Terrorist drag

This is perhaps one of the less well-known drag styles, but still uber-important to point out. The term "Terrorist drag" was coined by José Esteban Muñoz, author of the book *Disidentifications*, as a reflection of the drag style that Vaginal Creme Davis (and others like Carmelita Tropicana) performed. Terrorist drag, perhaps even more so than Genderf**k drag, was a major F**k you to ALL the systems—including drag itself.

Terrorist drag embraces and celebrates the social threat of drag and the dismantling of all accepted systems and the term was used by Muñoz to distinguish drag artists who use drag to interrogate and amplify their otherness and showcase their discoveries in their clothing, style, and performance choices.

Terrorist drag artists, more than a distinctive manner of dress, have distinctive ways in which they express and perform. More often than not, their costume style is that of Genderf**k drag but includes intentionally woven-in artistic self-explorations and reflections that may or may not leave audiences feeling uncomfortable. It is perhaps the style furthest away from mainstream drag, but the closest to its original intention.

If Terrorist drag interests you (as it does me), I highly recommend you check out Muñoz's book in the bonus Resources section (see page 139.)

Deliciousness

Genderf**k

I love Genderf**k drag A LOT! This style is a direct and exact reflection of its name—it is intended to subvert the gender norms, intentionally blurring gender lines by consciously choosing items of clothing that are meant to confuse audiences.

Because of the perceived "three articles" requirement in the1950s and '60s, this style of drag was popular as it allowed our LGBTQIA+ community to keep from getting arrested by mixing some gender-appropriate clothing in with their drag. Drag artists would mix skirts with tuxedos, football jerseys with heels—anything that intentionally gave off a big F**k you to gender norms.

One of my favorite examples of this is glam rock and its pioneers, David Bowie and Brian Eno.

Queerlesque

Queerlesque is a relatively new merging of drag and burlesque, which has come to mean burlesque for the queer community, and the queering of the burlesque community.

Much of this crossover begins in another queer-friendly off-shoot of burlesque called neo-burlesque, but with queerlesque the bridging of the two art forms was intentionally created by and for queer folxs as a performative vehicle to explore queer bodies, history, and all the fabulousness that happens in between. Queerlesque offers up a safe space for ALL queer artists to explore their bodies, sexuality, identity, (dis)ability, and performance in spaces where there are others who are like them.

A queerlesque performance typically offers up some kind of reveal, whether stripping or another visible deconstruction like de-dragging onstage. Costumes lean toward a more genderf**k version of traditional burlesque, with male-presenting performers in heels, and hyper-feminization and masculinization of all gender performers.

Queerlesque shows and festivals have popped up all over the world. I recommend finding and attending one; they are a lot of fun and their numbers are always fierce!

Opposite: Queerlesque in Palermo, Italy.

FIERCE *Drag* ADVICE

Loving learning all about the many styles of drag?
Want more juicy drag details and drag examples?
I've gotcha covered! For a more up close and
personal look into some of the drag styles, check
out the Drag Profiles of some of my favorite
artists scattered throughout this book—they
won't disappoint!

And if you're feeling a bit overwhelmed with
all the fierceness thrown at ya or if all this drag
is new to you, I've got you covered there too.
I've created a quick reference guide to all the
drag styles (and a few more!) that you
just learned about.

DRAGCAP

GURL! *snaps fan open and starts fanning self* We *clap* have *clap* traveled, hunty!

A Dragcap is something I introduced in my book, *How to Be a Drag Queen*, to help us integrate, digest, and allow all the glitter of information to settle—and bake. Because this book packs a big girl punch when it comes to content and sharing all the goods, I've included a Dragcap in each chapter of this one too. So let the baking and capping begin!

In this first chapter, we've gone all around the drag world to discover the different drag styles and identities in order to answer the question, "What is drag?" While there are never clear-cut answers in any art form—especially drag—we've revealed some things that are definitely worth tucking into our drag bag for the remainder of our journey. Here's a list of our most important discoveries so far:

• We dived deep into all the definitions, styles, and terminology of what drag is.

• We learned about the drag element of camp and how it's used to queer things up.

• We sauntered down a list of many of the different styles of drag.

• You now have a sickening cheat sheet of drag terminology that you can refer back to whenever you need a quick refresh.

Now it's your turn. You're here reading this book for a reason. Whatever that reason is, the only way to truly know something—drag included—is to put yourself in the thick of it. To experience it yourself (spoiler alert: that's coming too!). You've had a moment to read, learn, discover, and now take yourself through your first Dragcap. After all this I want to know, what is drag to you?

You've read my own and others' definitions of drag; what's yours? What are you still curious about? Which drag styles and identities do you want to learn more about? Take a moment to jot your thoughts down on the pages provided overleaf, on your phone, or in a notebook. We do this in the spirit and hopes of creating many more definitions for ourselves as we move in, through, and out of this book into our everyday magical lives!

Like drag, this book is interactive. Because I don't just want you to just read about all this fierceness and glam, **_I want you to become and embody it all too._**

Up next... Now that we have a fuller understanding of the grandness of drag as an art form, we're turning our lashed and stashed sights on to another set of questions.

• Where did drag start?

• Where did drag come from?

• Who was the first drag queen?

All this—and more!—is coming to you in the next chapter!

What is drag to you?

DRAG *Queen* PROFILE

The Legendary Tommie Ross

You really can't introduce Tommie Ross to the stage (or this book) without prefacing her name with the word "legendary." That's because more than any queen I know, she is deserving, worthy, and exemplary of that status. I've been blessed to know, perform in, and judge Miss Gay USofA 2019 (as well as many other pageants including Miss USofA Diva) alongside Tommie for the last decade and I've chosen to profile her over the many other drag queens possible because her story is unrivaled. Allow me to introduce you to your new favorite queen!

Name: Tommie Ross

Location: Dallas, TX, but international drag queen of the world.

Titles: Everything. Tommie is one of the most decorated queens in the biz with a whopping nine national drag titles.

Most iconic drag moment: Any time she hits the stage.

She has been known to make surprising entrances from the top of a staircase and other untapped dramatically drag entryways. She is notorious for using her ruffle cover-ups as a rug to lay on while she slays the kids with her lip-synch and watches the audience line up to tip her BIG. It's so flawless to watch!

Most iconic impersonations: One of my favorite impersonations she does is Erykah Badu. In her iconic performance, she recreates Badu's look from headwrap to big jewelry to seductive and mystical attitude. (Spoiler alert: you can find a library of her doing this gig on YouTube by Googling her and Badu's name!)

Where you can find her: You can find her on Facebook: facebook.com/tommieross4ever

DRAG *King* PROFILE

Pecs

Pecs is a UK drag king collective that was founded by actor and playwright Temi Wilkey (who is no longer with the collective) and freelance theater director Celine Lowenthal in 2013. They have been featured in *Vice Magazine*, *Time Out*, *LondonTheater1*, and now here! According to their website, they are an "all female/non-binary theatre and cabaret company." [2] This profile features not one, not two, but EIGHT diverse Kings of the ball!

Name: Pecs

Who: At the time of writing, the cast of Pecs includes Scott Free, Thrustin Limbersnake, Loose Willis, Izzy Aman, Victor Victorious, Mr. Goldenballs, John Travulva, and Johnny Gash.

Location: UK

What they offer: In addition to sold-out shows, Pecs also offers Mansformation workshops on developing your drag character for trans and nonbinary folk. You can also listen to the kings talk all things Drag Kings on their podcast The Drag King Cast.

Where you can find them: Website pecsdragkings.com and on Instagram @pecsdragkings

THE BIRTH OF DRAG

*S*o where did all this glamour and drama begin? How and why did it start in the first place? And where did the term "drag" originate? We're going to dive deeper into all of drag's humble beginnings in this chapter. But before we do, I always like to preface any talks about drag history with this rhinestone caveat:

When it comes to drag, there is a lot more we don't know than we do know.

Why? Because as marginalized people, most of our lineages and histories are oral and performative, meaning that drag lives on the stage and at the moment it is happening. Most of the drag history we do know is based on recounted stories, pieced-together timelines, and historical events that often only focus on select areas—San Francisco and New York in the USA, and London in the UK.

Drag's narrative is still being written as independent scholars, drag lovers, and researchers continue to mine their local history for their own origin stories to add to the collective narrative. I did this in 2018 when I took it upon myself to research, collect, and write about the history and evolution of drag in Dallas, Texas (you can find the article in the Resources section, page 140.)

Opposite: Drag queens in Soho, London

The story I wrote is only one story, in one city, out of thousands, which means we have so much further to go. Our history—or "dragstory" is only as complete as those who take the initiative to record it. And the only way we will ever know our story fully is for individuals to continue to research, document, and share their local drag history so we can begin piecing together our collective one. Until that glorious reconstruction day comes, let's take a saunter down some of the collective history we do know.

Let's start by taking a look at the term "drag."

According to the Oxford English Dictionary, the word "drag" has been in our vernacular since the late 1300s. But it wasn't until the 1800s that drag's meaning began to take shape into what we know it as today.

The meaning of drag that we have come to know in the US has roots in theater, particularly Shakespearean theater. A look at the etymology of the term drag on etymology.com places our modern-day definition of drag, i.e. wearing and performing in the clothes of one's gender opposite, as rooted in 1870s theater slang. [3]

On May 29th, 1870, as recorded in the 1890s book *Slang and Its Analogues Past and Present Volume 2*, the

British *Reynold's News* newspaper published what perhaps might be the first recorded usage of the term drag in a gender-bending context in their "Police Proceedings":

"He afterwards said, that instead of having a musical party he thought he would make it a little fancy dress affair, and said, **we shall come in DRAG, which means men wearing women's costumes**." (emphasis mine) [4]

The most common and well-known origins of modern-day drag are rooted in Elizabethan theater, when cis-gender women were not allowed on stage and cis-men played every single role. As part of their gender-opposite performance, cis-men would often wear petticoats and long ball gowns which would drag along the floor behind them as they moved around the stage, hence the birth of the terms "drag" and "dragging."

While a full exploration of drag's global history is beyond the scope of this little book, I do want to point out that outside of Shakespearean theater this men-dressed-as-women misogynistic form of drag took place elsewhere in the world too, such as in the theaters of ancient Greece where cis-gender men used masks to play female roles.

In the Japanese dance-drama form Kabuki, the Kabuki troupe was originally all female, with cis-women playing both female and male roles, until women were banned

from the stage in 1629 and the all-male present-day version was born.

These are all important timestamps in drag's history, because they show a global historical misogyny that has since tainted drag's history and is also an issue that modern-day drag is still (and often) accused of.

By the 1860s, despite some continuing prejudice against women who acted on theater stages, cis-gender women performing as male impersonators (what we call drag kings today) were making a mark in music halls around the globe, but particularly in Britain.

Drag kings, as we know them today, first appeared on stage in the 17th-century British tradition of pantomime, in which the leading male character and his romantic partner were both played by women, the former in men's clothing. The "Dame," the older female role in the production, was usually also played by a man in drag (thus perhaps making the British pantomime one of the only, if not the original, entertainment in which both men and women performed in drag together on the same stage.) The drag king also rose to mainstream culture via British music hall and

Opposite: A male actor takes the role of a geisha in Kabuki

American variety theaters, where women appeared dressed as dapper men, performing monologues, singing, and dancing—much more like the drag shows we see today.

We know even less about the history of our AFAB and female drag queen counterparts. While I began, in my first book, tracing our drag lineage back to the hyper-feminization of 1950s movie stars and the concept of Masquerade—particularly in Bette Davis' film persona of Miss Moffat in the movie of the same name—we are nowhere near even scratching the surface of our roots in drag.

FIERCE *Drag* FACT

Despite popular belief, the term drag is not an acronym for Dressed As Girl. This is a mistake that has been made by many a drag queen including Ru herself. The origin of this myth is also linked back to the Shakespearean period, but word and language etymology shows acronyms didn't come into general vernacular use until the 20th century—hundreds of years AFTER Shakespeare's time. #debunked

Opposite: A pantomime dame

DRAG PROFILE

A Tale of Firsts

In this special edition of our Drag Profiles, I thought it would be fun to take a look at all the "firsts" in drag (well, at least as we know them today). From the very first drag queen and king, I hope that these profiles prompt you to learn more about the pioneers of our dragstory.

Princess Seraphina

Year: Early 18th century

Drag: Queen

Story: Born John Cooper, Princess Seraphina was the first recorded drag queen in English history. He rose to notoriety when he took a friend to court for stealing his clothes in 1732 and was a self-proclaimed molly (gay man).

ANNIE HINDLE

Annie Hindle*

Year: c.1840–1904

Drag: King

Story: Annie Hindle began performing at the age of six and by her twenties, she had appeared in musical halls all over England. Eventually making her way to the United States, Annie was billed as "The Great Impersonator of Male Character." While she was known for her solo act and unrivaled stardom and talent at the time, Annie (like Julian Eltinge, below) also performed in racist minstrel shows.

William Dorsey Swann

Year: 1858–1925

Drag: Queen

Story: So much of Swann's history has been discovered thanks to the work and research of Channing Gerard Joseph. Swann was born a slave in Maryland and was freed in 1863. In the 1880s, he organized the first drag balls in Washington DC. In April 1888, the police raided one of his balls, in the first documented case in the United States of folxs being arrested for drag. According to Joseph's research, Swann was also the first American activist taking legal action to fight for the rights of our queer community. Swann proclaimed himself the "Queen of Drag" and if we are looking for the origins of our modern-day drag movement, Swann and the Ball culture (see page 46) are it.

Julian Eltinge*

Year: 1881–1941
Drag: Female impersonation
Story: Frank DeCaro and others often point to Julian
Eltinge as being the first example of modern day drag.
However, the research differs. Eltinge was a cis-gender
heterosexual white man who performed as a female on
stage (often in the racist Cohan & Harris minstrel shows)
and was uber-protective of his masculinity off it—what
today we would call toxic masculinity. And while there's
no denying that Eltinge did play a role in popularizing
female impersonation (note my conscious decision not
to call him a drag queen) as a comedic trope, as far as
our queer community is concerned, he really contributed
nothing else.

Gladys Bentley aka Barbara "Bobbie" Minton

Year: 1907–1960

Drag: King

Story: Gladys's career began when she moved to New York at the age of 16 and answered the call of a notoriously gay speakeasy's need for a piano player. It was here that Gladys found her signature fly style of tuxedos and suits that would mark her legacy as one of the most important and prominent Black queer figures to emerge during the Harlem Renaissance.

* Both Annie and Julian are included on this list as a reference and checkpoint that drag, in addition to misogyny, has racist roots. Racism is often bypassed and overlooked when writing about the origins of drag and my radical drag heart wanted to make sure this book didn't do the same.

AMERICAS GREATEST SEPIA PIANA ARTIST

BROWN BOMBER OF SOPHISTICATED SONGS

Gladys Bentley

*T*heaters and movies are usually where scholars and researchers immediately go looking for the origin and history of drag, but as Swann's story shows, drag in the form of underground balls has been around since the 1800s. Because balls were specific to the Black queer community and racism was outright and legal, records of the origins of drag outside—and before—the silver screen are few and hard to find.

There was so much that was happening in our community, off the silver screen, and, luckily for us, there are new generations of BIPOC, queer, and Intersectional drag artists who are deeply committed to researching, recording, and understanding drag's roots outside of this traditional mainstream perspective. The real tea is, we were writing our own history way before the history books caught up with us.

Often in my writings and *pláticas* on the history of drag, I'll break our origin story into two parts. The first is the history of drag in theater, movies, and comedic tropes. I refer to this as the heterosexual origins of drag, which we just covered. While this is one part of the story, it is not **THE** story. It is not **OUR** story.

That belongs to us. And our queer history is the part we will now focus on—what I often refer to as drag's queer origins. Because our real story originates with brave individuals like William Dorsey Swann, for whom drag was an expression and extension of themselves, not a trope they put on out of misogyny, or for money, laughs, or fame.

OUR QUEER DRAG
Timeline

Because drag history can get a bit overwhelming, I wanted to share it in a way that every dragster could get behind, a timeline! Here you'll find key historical moments throughout drag's evolution from our queer perspective. Please keep in mind as you read through it that this is far from an all-inclusive list—that could fill a whole book! This list highlights the moments, people, and events that set the legacy of drag as we know it today in motion. Let's begin!

1858
William Dorsey Swann

The first self-proclaimed queen of drag, queer activist, and the birth of the modern-day drag movement (see page 76.)

1870
Drag becomes part of our lexicon

Drag in its queer meaning of men dressing in women's clothes became part of our vernacular for the first time via the UK's *Reynolds News* as captured in Volume Two of *Slang and Its Analogues Past and Present* (see page 68.)

1920s
Drag Ball Culture

As we've seen above, the first drag balls were thrown by William Dorsey Swann in the 1880s. While ball culture persisted after Swann's death, the version that still exists today found its groove during the Harlem Renaissance and birthed historical drag legends like Gladys Bentley (see Drag Profile: A Tale of Firsts, page 78.)

1965

The Imperial Court System

More than just a drag pageant, this is one of the oldest and the longest-running LGBTQIA+ organizations in the world. The Imperial Court System was founded by self-proclaimed Absolute Empress of San Francisco, José Sarria. There are various chapters throughout the USA, Canada, and Mexico. In its early years, there was some crossover with the Ball Community. The system is still going strong today and hosts coronations, where new monarchs and royalty are crowned.

1969

Stonewall Riots

It took an entire village to uprise and defeat the system. That village included the entire spectrum of our diversity. For more about the history of PRIDE and the riots read *The Little Book of Pride* by Lewis Laney (see Resources, page 139.)

1972
Pink Flamingos

One of the most iconic queer duos in our history, Divine and John Waters, both played an important role in queering their respective genres, as first seen in the movie *Pink Flamingos*. Up until Waters' movies, drag was only known only through heterosexual comedic drag tropes via movies such as *Some Like It Hot*. None of the mainstream movies coming out at the time truly captured drag's queer essence until Waters and Divine entered the arena.

1972

Miss Gay America

Miss Gay America was started by Norma Kristie (aka Norman Jones) in Nashville, Tennessee at what was then The Watch Your Hat and Coat Saloon. Miss Gay America is a pageant that adheres to strict gender rules where all contestants must be born as male and have no augmentation. This system and five contestants were the subject of the 2008 documentary film, *Pageant*.

1979
Sisters of Perpetual Indulgence

Since its beginning on Easter Sunday of 1979, the Sisters have created chapters worldwide including in Germany, the UK, Uruguay, and Colombia. They are founded upon community service and outreach and use "humor and irreverent wit to expose the forces of bigotry, complacency, and guilt that chain the human spirit." [5]

1980
Miss Continental

Founded by Jim Flint, this elite pageant system is open to transwomen drag queens as well as AMAB drag queens. This system was created partially in response to the need and desire for transwomen to compete in pageants and the lack of opportunities for them to do so.

1985
Wigstock

This was the first attempt at taking a drag show mainstream and, unbeknownst to itself, would also set the stage and template for "RuPaul's Drag Race." It was also the first open invite to the public to catch a glimpse of the glitter and glam that was raging on in gay bars around London and the US. Wigstock ran for 12 years, became a documentary film of the same name on their 10-year anniversary in 1995, and came back full throttle as a cruise in 2015.

FIERCE *Drag* FACT

Jennie Livingston was a consulting producer for Ryan Murphy's "Pose," which was a fictional but very real and representational take on the Black Queer Ball community.

1986
Miss Gay USofA

Miss Gay USofA was created by Jerry Bird with the crowning of Michael Andrews. Miss Gay USofA would go on to be the first of the "big three" pageant systems to include the spectrum of drag under its umbrella. There are now nine divisions of Miss Gay USofA including Miss USofA Diva founded in 2014, and Mr Gay USofA and Mister USofA MI, both founded in 2008.

1990
Paris is Burning

Around the same year as Wigstock was being billed as the world's first drag festival, an NYU film student named Jennie Livingston was spending time filming drag balls and getting to know the NYC Ball community intimately. The resulting documentary, *Paris is Burning*, would bring Ball Culture to the mainstream and quickly became an iconic queer film.

1995

The Faux Queen Pageant

This was the first pageant 100% dedicated to faux queens, female drag queens, AFAB queens, and hyper queens.

1999

International Drag King Extravaganza (IDKE)

International Drag King Extravaganza was the first event and festival of its kind to center on and feature drag kings. The first IDKE festival took place in October 1999 in Columbus, Ohio, and was founded by four drag kings— Julie Applegate (Jake), Shani Scott (Maxwell), Sile Singleton (Luster/Lustivious de la Virgion), and Donna Troka (DJ love)—and other Columbus LGBTQIA+ members.

Opposite: Alaya Richman performs at IDKE in Cleveland, Ohio

2001
Bio Queen Manifesto

This was a public letter conceived by four female drag queens, Summer's Eve, Kentucky Fried Woman, Miss Triss, and Venus Envy, and read at the third annual IDKE. So far in my research this is the first public proclamation and manifesto for our style of drag.

2009
"RuPaul's Drag Race" airs

The rest is history.

We'll pick up drag's history in our next chapter, "Drag Today," but as you can see from this snapshot, drag has a rich and diverse history outside of heteronormative theater and movies. So much PRIDE, evolution, and brave fights for equality. We have come so far. And it's deeply exciting to see where we'll go next!

Draaama **93**

DRAGCAP

FRIEEENDS!! We've gathered a lot of knowledge about the origins of drag. And you want to know what's really crazy? It's that what you've learned about here is only a small fraction of what our full dragstory is. New stories, research, and people will continue to be uncovered as more and more folxs get curious about getting a 360-degree view of drag's history.

Until that glorious day comes, let's dive into a quick Dragcap of all the drama of this chapter.

• We've discovered the first usage of the term drag, and debunked a decades-long drag myth!

• We've gotten clear on drag's history but also how our community is rewriting that history.

• We've learned about some of the first queens and kings of drag.

• And we've got a sickening timeline of our queer drag history that you can refer back to and add to as you continue your own adventures and research in this wonderful world of drag.

After reading this chapter, you know a lot more about the history of drag than some queens, kings, and royalty in-betweens gracing the stage. So what are you going to do with this knowledge?

My hope is that you will share it with everyone you know. Because that's how drag continues to evolve. The legacy of drag changes to meet the ever-evolving needs and desires of the audience, but also the changes in and introduction of new technologies and, most importantly, the evolution of the people who perform drag.

For those of you who might be historical geeks like me and can't get enough of all this drag origin talk, I've created a list full of books and articles to help kick off your own research! Some of these books are out of print, but most can be found at your favorite indie bookstore! You'll find all this amazingness in the Resources section (pages 138–141.)

Up next...

Dust off your favorite PRIDE outfit, because it's time for a celebration! We are family and in this next chapter, we are going to dance our way through the fabulousness of what drag is today and get a sneak peek of where drag might be strutting down the runway next.

DRAG PROFILE

Female Drag Queen

Fauxnique

Back in the early 2000s when I first started discovering my drag self and researching if there were other AFAB queens like me, one name kept popping up over and over again: Fauxnique. Since then, as with many of the artists profiled in this book, I have had the pleasure and honor to call her my friend. She was a female drag queen before female drag was cool. And I'm so excited to share her dopeness with you!

Name: Fauxnique

Location: San Francisco, California, USA

Drag: Female, AFAB, Queen

Title: Fauxnique was the first cis-woman to win San Francisco's annual Trannyshack competition in 2003.

Story: Fauxnique has been making silent history for decades. A trained ballerina and fierce artist, she has created her own one-woman shows like The F Word, C*NT, or The Horror of Nothing To See, and has performed her Beautility piece at San Francisco's City Hall. She is also the author of *Faux Queen: A Life In Drag* (see Resources, page 138.)

Where you can find her: fauxnique.net and on Instagram @moniquefauxnique

Drag Family

DRAG TODAY

"We are family!"

It's a song, a phrase, and an ethos that we queers live, breathe, and drag by. It's blown through speakers on floats in just about every PRIDE parade there is. And it's always a crowd-pleaser whenever a queen takes the stage and belts out this gay anthem. It's also the spirit that we see invoked as we begin to make drag our own—and make it a show!

Up until now, we've been seeing drag in the rear-view mirror, looking back to try and capture the realness of this wonderland of drag and what makes it so amazing today. In this chapter, we are going to turn the mirror on our own fabulous, mugged-up selves and see how we are living, creating, and dragging our queer art form into the history books now.

Hold on to your wigs, stashes, and lashes, hunties! We are in for an epically bumpy but fabulous ride!

Today, we can't turn on our TVs or scroll through Instagram without seeing a drag queen somewhere in the mix. Drag has managed to evolve from dive bars to the Las Vegas stage, with *RuPaul's Drag Race Live* at the Flamingo Hotel. We've seen drag queens in the 2018 Virgin Atlantic Pride flight commercial. Shangela and Willam were Lady Gaga's entourage in *A Star is Born* and dozens of queens have performed on stage alongside some of the biggest pop stars of our time, such as Katy Perry and Miley Cyrus.

We've seen drag queens as bartenders on Andy Cohen's "Watch What Happens Live." We've even seen Alyssa Edwards slaying the kids with her very own Netflix television show, "Dancing Queen," and as the face of Tazo® Tea and head of the very first Camp Tazo®.

So what prompted this massive growth spurt? A little BIG drag show named "RuPaul's Drag Race."

It was clear from the outset that RuPaul was destined to change the course of drag. From his involvement with Lady Bunny in Wigstock to his self-proclamation and self-titled 1993 debut album *RuPaul: Supermodel of the World*, RuPaul had the makings of a pop culture icon from the beginning. Coming from a club kid and almost Terrorist drag background, RuPaul found a way to take his love and passion for drag and turn it into his business.

(Although out of print, one of the best reads of RuPaul's history pre-Drag Race is his autobiography, *Lettin It All Hang Out*, published in 1995.)

"RuPaul's Drag Race" premiered in the USA in 2009 on Logo TV and crowned its first winner, BeBe Zahara Benet, in what is often referred to as the Lost Season. Since its premiere, the show has been syndicated all over the world including in Chile, Thailand, New Zealand, and the Philippines, to name a few. Not to mention all the spin-offs like "Drag U" and "RuPaul's Drag Con" that it has produced. Over the course of three decades, RuPaul has taken his career, and his drag, from playing punk clubs in Atlanta to having the most Emmys wins (11) for a Black Artist, to launching hundreds of careers, to opening a show in Vegas, to having his own class, RuPaul Teaches Self-Expression and Authenticity, in the Masterclass online learning series.

But glory is not without its backlash. RuPaul has been facing a current of his own for some of his statements and belief about what constitutes drag. And because drag has always responded to adversity by showing up and showing out, a plethora of new, diverse drag shows, events, and festivals have emerged, such as the 2014 Austin

International Drag Festival. The festival features a variety of drag artists like kings, Gender***ers, and female drag queens over four nights in various clubs throughout Austin, Texas. During the day festival goers can choose from a variety of drag, make-up, and performance workshops.

Another all-inclusive drag pageant was started in 2019 by former "RuPaul's Drag Race" alumni Alaska. Her Drag Queen of the Year Pageant has crowned two diverse drag winners—the first a goth drag artist and the second a drag king.

Perhaps one of the biggest and most successful shows to emerge is The Boulet Brothers', "Dragula," which focuses on more underground, diverse, and gothic and punk rock Genderf**k styles of drag. They self-produced the first season in 2016 on the YouTube channel Hey Qween where it was picked up by Canadian OutTV and stayed for two seasons. "Dragula" has made history not only because of its focus on a more underground style of drag, but also for the diversity of its contestants (something that "Drag Race" has been publicly criticized about), who include the first drag king, Landon Cider, who won season three, and the first female drag queen, Sigourney Beaver, in their 2021 season.

These are just two of the plethora of shows that have sprung up in response to—and perhaps because of—the lack of diversity and representation in "RuPaul's Drag Race." More—such as "Camp Wannakiki"—are popping up online all the time.

A big part of drag's mainstreaming has not necessarily been what we see on our TV and computer screens, but the wide variety of events that are welcoming drag queens. Pre-Covid, local libraries all over the states started Drag Queen Story Hour with huge success—and of course some backlash. Drag queens would pick their favorite books about diversity and inclusivity and slay the kids with their readings. Drag brunches have popped up in Virgin Hotels and in art-centered neighborhoods and restaurants. It's safe to say drag is everywhere.

Looking at the progression from where drag has been to where it is now, it's easy for audiences and our community to say, "We've made it!" While that is definitely true, we still have a long way to go!

Opposite: Drag Queen Story Hour has been a huge success

DRAG PROFILE

Drag Youth

Desmond Is Amazing

One of the most beautiful things that drag going mainstream has ushered in is a deeper acceptance—and not just tolerance—of LGBTQIA+ folxs. And that love and acceptance have made their way down to the place that needs the support, love, and understanding the most—our youth. There is just so much to love about this story, humxn, and profile. I was introduced to Desmond Is Amazing early in my own drag research when I found him on Instagram #beforehewasfamous and I have been a follower and fan ever since!

Name: Desmond Is Amazing

Drag: Genderf**k

Story: Desmond was born in 2007 and began their drag career at the age of eleven. Since traveling the drag circuit (with their parents of course), Desmond's drag

career really began to bloom when they were a speaker
at the 2017 PRIDE Rally. They have since gone on to host
the kids' fashion show at RuPaul's Drag Con; they were
a speaker at the Teen Vogue Summit; and they authored
the book *Be Amazing* (see page 138), and launched
their first single, "We Are Amazing," on April 30, 2021.
Desmond Is Amazing is currently launching their own media
networks for LGBTQIA+ youth! Desmond Is Amazing and
their contribution to drag and our community truly are
outrageously amazing!

Where you can find them: desmondisamazing.com and
on IG @desmondisamazing

*I*t's not just our youth who are experiencing the joy and benefits of drag's accessibility, we all are! Thanks to YouTube, Instagram, and all other forms of social media, drag has been made accessible all over the world. Pair that with "RuPaul's Drag Race" international franchises, and drag has never been more available and easy to access. This new accessibility at your fingertips has created not just a whole new stage for drag where one doesn't even need to leave their house to drag, but also new forms such as Instadrag—Look Queens who produce various drag looks and photoshoots for Instagram, drag make-up tutorials, and drag online workshops which are are popping up everywhere.

Even social media and celebrity TV have gotten their drag on. TikTok is basically a drag app for non-drag folxs (and some drag ones) and the popular show "Lip Synch Battle" pairs two celebrities against each other—often they will dress in drag to perform (check out one of my favorites, Joseph Gordon-Levitt's *Rhythm Nation* performance. E P I C!).

With this ease and accessibility, drag is once again evolving. And with all this goodness, growth, and momentum, the big question now becomes, where else is there for drag to go? *Can drag go anywhere else?*

One of my personal intentions and hopes as I continue to do the work and perform as a drag artist is that drag will evolve to be a more inclusive and more wide-reaching representation of ALL of us—in mainstream media and in our community. Because if drag is going to evolve anywhere, it's going to be toward a more radically inclusive representation of our queer rainbow. Or maybe drag will evolve back to its radical roots and we will once again find ourselves using our bodies and our queer art as vehicles for protest.

Anything and everything is possible! And guess what? It all can (and does!) start with us!

DRAG *Icon* PROFILE

Divine

Out of all the queens past and present, Divine has always held a special place in my drag heart. Divine was an original. A one-of-a-kind and a once-in-a-lifetime experience. Hailed as the Drag Queen of the Century by *Time* magazine in 1988, Divine met John Waters, who lived down the street from him, at 16. They started making movie magic in 1966 and 1968 with two short films titled *Roman Candles* and *Eat Your Make-up*. But it was their 1972 collaboration in the film *Pink Flamingos* (see page 85) that set Divine on the path to legendary status.

Pink Flamingos, while not for the faint of heart, was the best that cult cinema and cult drag had to offer. It was camp, kitsch, perverse, disturbing, and subversive. Which made it great. And it solidified Divine as a cult icon who would do whatever it took to make a sickening movie.

In the 1970s and '80s Divine recorded club music, with his biggest hit, "You Think You're a Man," landing him an appearance on the UK television show "Top of the Pops."

But just as Divine was going to make his mainstream crossover debut in a recurring role in "Married… With Children," he died of a heart attack on March 7, 1988.

DRAGCAP

ROYAAALS! Let's celebrate how far we've come!
In this chapter, we discovered that not only are we family, but we are fiercely charting new waves and creating our own oceans of flawlessness and possibility. Here is a quick snapshot of all the things we've learned!

• We've seen how "RuPaul's Drag Race" has opened doors for new and diverse drag shows.

• We've learned about how those shows are making drag history.

• We've learned about some fierce drag kids and one amazing drag icon.

• Finally, we've dreamt of some of the places drag can go—and grow!

Up next... In our final chapter, we're going to bring all the glamor, glitter, fabulousness, and fame back around to you! We'll have a kiki about some of the best elements to emerge from drag's entering the spotlight, and then turn that spotlight on you. That's right, fierce beings.

You are being served up next!

DRAG FAMILY

Part Deux

DRAG AND YOU!

The Dragolution is here, hunties!! And you are a part of it! This book is a part of it. We ALL are a part of it.

Take a look around—at your TV, the latest magazine, award shows, your favorite streaming services, and bookstores. Drag is in the prime of its life and if you really want to know what's next for drag, just take a look around. Because we are living the grandness NOW.

We are seeing so many new shows, books, stories, and festivals being birthed as a direct result and response to how fast drag is growing. But through all the growth spurts, what we've discovered as we've sashayed along is that drag's rise to fame isn't something that drag's fairy godmother whipped up overnight. It was a long, slow, steady build that, yes, has been spurred on by the popularity of "RuPaul's Drag Race," but was really birthed from a community that needed a break from the realness of life. Drag rose from the ashes of a community that was persecuted because they were born to love, look, express, define, and act differently.

Drag has always been a part of us. And we have always been a part of drag's legacy. The only thing different now is that we are inviting others in. Whether that's through Emmy Award-winning Shows, websites, Vegas cabarets, or good old-fashioned bar shows, we've welcomed a whole new generation of audiences into our fabulous little queer world. With drag becoming accessible to all through movies, shows, and social media, we're seeing more and more people enter onto the drag scene.

Drag has made the world a better place. And we're experiencing more diversity and equality because of it.

I'll never forget the immense amount of possibility I felt in my spirit as I first watched Aaron Davis perform. I knew in a heartbeat and without any second-guessing that drag was my home. Maybe, after reading about all the glitz and glam in this book, you feel that way too? Or maybe you felt that way long before you picked up this book or watched your first episode of "Drag Race." Maybe, like me, you see a piece or the whole of yourself reflected in drag. And maybe, just maybe, you're finally feeling fierce enough to try it.

Well guess what daaahlings?!?! If all this fundamental reading has gotten your little drag heart pumping, excited, and itching to try drag on for yourself, you're in for an uber special treat! Because as our last and final adventure together in this wonderland of drag, we're going to pass the mic to beautiful, irreplaceable, and flawless YOU!

DRAG PROFILE

You!

So you want to be a drag queen? King? Artist? Or maybe something radically different and in-between? Perhaps all this reading about the sparkle of others has got you itching to find a drag shimmer that's all your own? Well in our final Drag Profile, we are spotlighting you—as in your possible future drag self!

I love helping folxs get started in drag so much that I actually wrote an entire book about it called *How to Be a Drag Queen: A guidebook for female drag queens and emerging drag artists* (see Resources, page 140.) Below, I'm going to share with you my top seven tips to follow if you want to get started in drag. Let the drag games begin!

Drag Tip no.1

Know what you're getting into

By that I mean, know the story, history, fundamentals, and legacy of the variant of the form you're wanting to venture into. You're already a bazillion steps ahead because you picked up this book and made it this far (unless you skipped ahead to this part, in which case, go back and catch up on what you missed *wink*).

A couple of practical tips on how to do this:

• Get to know your local drag artists. Chances are that wherever you are located there are tons of local drag artists who have been where you want to be. Take a moment to get to know them. Share their shows. DM them and let them know you are wanting to do drag and ask if you could help them carry their bags at the next show or anything else they might need. This is exactly how I got started in drag many, many moons ago.

• Know your drag history—local and global. This book has you covered on the latter but take some time to research the local legends in your area.

Drag Family Part Deux **121**

Drag Tip no.2

Know yourself

This is such a fundamental element of life and drag, that even RuPaul himself emphasizes this tip on every season of "Drag Race." That's because if you don't know who you are and what you want, you'll be at the mercy of whichever way the wind, world, society, or drag wants to take you. And drag is about personal, creative, and expressive agency.

In order to be the best drag artist you can be, you've got to know yourself well enough to steward your way through drag. Otherwise, you're just expressing and creating someone else's dream, vision, and belief about what drag is. But you also have to be malleable enough to learn as you grow, and brave enough to implement what you're learning on the go. Because drag is also a vehicle to get to know and grow into yourself. It's a beautiful space of both/and, where you don't have to choose between one thing or another, but can embody both those things (and more) at once. But in order for drag's magic to help you discover who you are, you first have to know why you want to drag before diving in.

A couple of practical tips on how to do this:

• Start with the end in mind. What are your reasons for wanting to do drag? Is it just for fun? Is it a creative and/or expressive outlet? Do you want to perform? Try out for "Dragula," "RuPaul's Drag Race," or Alaska's Drag Queen of the Year Pageant?

• Keep a Drag Journal. This tool is HUGE when you are first starting out (and really is a gamechanger throughout your drag career). This is the space where you'll record all your ideas, dreams, costume visions, performance ideas, and notes related to drag. Write down songs you love and which you think would make a great performance. Jot down your favorite drag artists and why you love them. This journal is YOUR drag lab.

Drag Tip no.3

Know the fundamentals

So much so that you could regurgitate them on command.
They are called fundamentals for a reason—because
they are fundamental to the art form. In music, you learn
the fundamentals of the instrument, reading music,
and standard rhythm and beats. In drag, you learn the
fundamentals of painting a drag mug, putting together
a cohesive performance, costume, and show.

A few practical tips on how to do this:

• Learn the fundamentals of drag make-up. This is
contouring, highlighting, lashes and stashes, blending, and
baking. Check out YouTube and even TikTok and IG Reels
for some awesome drag mug tutorials.

• Uncover what makes a good drag performance
SICKENING. Watch TONS of drag. Go to every drag show
you can get into. Check out drag pageants on YouTube.
Learn what makes audiences go crazy—and what leaves
the whole room flat.

• Make notes of everything you discover in your drag journal.

• Use what you've learned to create a sickening drag persona and performance.

Because you've taken the time and care to follow these first three Drag Tips, you'll be that much more fierce, confident, and sickening when you do hit the stage. That's what the next four tips are all about!

FIERCE *Drag* FACT

A lot of people want to skip the first three tips to get to all the "good stuff" like painting their mug, figuring out their drag persona and coming up with a name—they want to go straight to Instagram before understanding the who, what, and why they wanted to jump into drag in the first place. You're here reading this book, so I know you haven't made and won't make that mistake.

Drag Tip no.4

Create your drag persona
aka the "Fun Stuff"

This is where the rubber meets the road; where you take everything you've learned and begin to craft it into something that is fiercely reflective of you. Your drag persona or character is made up of so many elements of which the following are a few.

• Your drag name.

• Your music choices.

• Your drag style.

• Your drag identifiers.

• Your drag mug
(which should have a personality all its own).

• Your attitude aka "dragitude."

• Your performance style and energy. Or your decision to not perform and just be a flawless Look Queen.

As you create your drag persona, remember that every element in drag is in a dance with each of the others, and everything should come together to tell a story. But also remember that this amalgamation of all the different elements takes time. Give yourself some space and watch how magnificently your drag will unfold!

A few practical tips on how to do this:

• Choose your drag name. Some drag artists start their drag by picking a name. Some are then given the last name of their *haus* like I was given the last name Skyy by my dragmother Jenna Skyy. Others just pick something random that captures their drag heart and imagination and run with it.

• Pick a drag style. But know that you are not married to it—you can change it or evolve it at any time, but you have to start somewhere, so start with the style that drew you into drag in the first place.

• Find (or make) your drag costume. This has always been my favorite part—creating a costume to go with my performance. If you're not going to perform, then you'll still need a good tipping outfit (an outfit that you walk around in). This is the time to make that drag magic happen!

Drag Tip no.5
Test it out

Now that you've got everything in place, it's time to take your drag self on a test run. This test run can look like anything—going out to the club in drag, snapping some photos of your drag self, and introducing yourself to your InstaFam. Or if you've got the performance bug, then sign up for your local amateur show. Most clubs that host professional drag shows also host amateur nights where they feature up-and-coming drag stars. (Hint: that's you!)

However you decide to take your drag on a test drive, here are a few things to keep in mind.

• If you decide to do an amateur night, make sure you know the format to submit your music in ahead of time.

• Some clubs only take USBs. Some only take CDs. Some will just ask what song you're going to perform and find it on their set list for you. Also, bring a backup in whatever format they ask.

• Have fun. You've done the work. Now you're just sharing with the world what you've been working hard on behind the scenes. This is your time to shine. The spotlight is yours. ENJOY IT!

Drag Tip no.6
Reflect

After your first ventures out as a bona fide drag artist, take a moment to reflect (preferably in your drag journal) on how everything went. Like the first three tips, most drag artists skip this step and therefore they never really grow. You know those artists who seem to be stuck doing the same tired looks and performances again and again? Most of the time it comes back to not taking the time to keep honing, learning, and practicing their craft. But you won't make that mistake. *Right?!?!?*

Here are some questions to help guide your reflection:

• What was good?

• What was not so good?

• What could you do better?

• When did you have the most fun?

• What kind of compliments did you get?

• Did you get compared to any other artist? (This can be

both good and bad. Good because you can check out who they compared you to and see how you can channel the things they are good at and make it your own. Bad because you'll also need to put in a little more work on making sure that your drag is distinctively *you*.)

Drag Tip no.7
Repeat

Repeat over and over, until you find your groove, you find your signature drag mug, and you find what your drag persona wants to be and how it best expresses itself. This takes time and a lot of going back to the fundamentals, reflection, testing out, failing, and going back to the drawing board. Or maybe you're a "one and done" kind of drag artist. That's okay too. If that's the case, take this moment to celebrate the fierceness of you!

Whatever you decide, wherever your drag goes from here, **OWN IT!**

One last thing...

Before we shut down the library of all our fabulousness, there's one final love note I'd like to share with you.

As drag becomes more and more popular and more people are invited and show up to the party, there will be some folxs who don't believe you belong there, in the mix. Know that more often than not, those people aren't just being assholes, but most of them are protective of this art form that they love so much and its history.

As you've come to learn and know throughout this book, drag has a deeper meaning then just the superficial fantasy that is often portrayed on TV. Most of us in the community just want you to know that. And to know your history—especially if you're privileged (white, cis-gender, heterosexual) coming into our space. It's all about respect. And yes, that's a two-way street that isn't always traveled by queer folxs and queens—especially when it comes to AFAB drag queens.

Regardless, don't let them tell you what you can and cannot do. There will be people who say you can't do drag. I've been doing it for decades, hold titles, and have been asked to judge almost every single pageant there is, and

I still get told this. You'll hear the fighting and the trolling on the internet over answers to questions like…

"Can straight people do drag?"

"Can women do drag?"

The list goes on and on. Pay those trolls no mind. If you care enough to read this book, you belong here. Drag is for everyone because it is already a part of everyone. In the infamous words of RuPaul:

"You're born naked and the rest is drag."

DRAGCAP

Hello there, your royal highness! All you amazing Kings, Queens, and Royal In-betweens! You've made it! And while this is our very last Dragcap together *womp womp*, we still have a few more adventures to take!

In this chapter, you learned perhaps the most important lesson of this book, how to be a drag queen—or king, or royal in-between! But you wanna know the most important takeaway of this section? The most important drag-away is that we write our own history as we live it. So my, dahlings…*how will you choose to live your drag?*

Up next... It's all you, boo.

It's time to take your first steps out into the real world as a bonafide member of our drag family. You've put in the time and effort, walked a mile (or at least the last 134 pages) in our rhinestone heel shoes, and you've even tried drag for yourself! You are ready to step into your royal kingdom and death drop right alongside us.

What comes next is all up to you.

• You can continue your adventures in Dragland by trying out and researching all the things you've read about in this book.

• You can Google when the next drag show or drag brunch featuring your local queens, kings, and royal in-betweens is on, book a seat, bring a wad of ones, and be the best, most lively and engaged audience member your artists have ever seen.

• You can buy a ticket for the final night of your favorite drag pageant—that's when all the drag really levels up to epic proportions.

• Or you can begin to build your own drag persona, seek out your own stage, and write your own dragstory.

Wherever this glorious glitter-rainbow brick road takes you is exactly where you need to be.

What will your dragstory be?

Condragulations Hunty!

You've made it to the end of this book.

But every good drag artist knows that the ending is just one more opportunity to be even *more* sickening and take the audience's breath away. And while you may have come to the end of this book, you're at the very beginning of your drag adventure!

I'm not quite done with you yet though. Before you go, I've curated a collection of references and resources so you can begin to plan and plot out your next grand solo drag adventure!

You've got this. And I believe massively in you!

Now go forth and be the slay, flawlessly!

xo-b

Notes

1 (page 19) The Sisters of Perpetual Indulgence, Inc.: www.thesisters.org

2 (page 62) Pecs Drag Kings: www.pecsdragkings.com

3 (page 68) Etymology of drag: www.etymonline.com/word/drag

4 (page 69) Quote about the first use of "drag": *Slang and Its Analogues Past and Present* by John Stephen Farmer and William Ernest Henley (Routledge Kegan Paul, 1965)

5 (page 87) The Sisters of Perpetual Indulgence, Inc.: www.thesisters.org/

References & Resources

Ta-da! As promised, here is a collection of goodies to help you level up your drag knowledge and slay game. **Hint:** one of my personal favorite things is to comb through the resources sections in books and see if I can pick up any additional reads that might help me further slay!

Movies and documentaries

FtF: Female to Femme (2006)

How Do I Look? (2006)

I Am Divine (2013)

Pageant (2008)

Paris is Burning (1990)

Pink Flamingos (1972)

Venus Boyz (2002)

Books

Be Amazing by Desmond Is Amazing (Farrar, Straus and Giroux, 2020)

Drag: the Complete Story by Simon Doonan (Laurence King, 2019)

Faux Queen by Monique Jenkinson (Fauxnique) (Bywater Books, 2022)

Female Impersonation by Carole-Anne Tyler
   (Routledge, 2002)
Gender Trouble by Judith Butler (Routledge Classics, 2006)
House of Swann by Channing Gerard Joseph (due to
   publish 2022, www.channingjoseph.com)
How To Be a Drag Queen by Brandi Amara Skyy (2019)
Lettin it All Hang Out by RuPaul (Hyperion Books, 1995)
The Little Book of Pride by Lewis Laney (Dog 'n' Bone, 2020)
Miss Piggy's Guide to Life by Henry Beard (Alfred Knopf
   Inc., 1981)

Books for drag history lovers

Disidentifications by José Esteban Muñoz (University of
   Minnesota Press, 1999)
Faux Queens by Brandi Amara Skyy (2017, 2nd ed 2022)
The House of Swann by Channing Gerard Joseph (Yes, it's
   on here twice—details above.)
Mother Camp by Esther Newton (University of Chicago
   Press, 1979)

Articles for drag history lovers

"Drag for All: A brief history of the faux queen pageant"
   by Ruby Toosday, fauxqueenpageant.blogspot.com

"InQueery: Trixie Mattel breaks down the history of 'drag' "
by Trixie Mattel, them.us/story/inqueery-drag

"The Terrorist Drag of Vaginal Davis" by Cyrus Grace
Dunham, newyorker.com/culture/culture-desk/terrorist-
drag-vaginal-davis

Books and articles by the author

The Drag Show Podcast. Interviews with drag artists on a
broad range of drag topics.

Faux Queens (2016)

"From Queen to Queer: the evolution of drag in Dallas."
dallasvoice.com/from-queen-to-queer-the-evolution-of-
drag-in-dallas

GAG Magazine 2013–2017. The first haute drag magazine.

How To Be a Drag Queen (2019)

"Walk, Burn, Pose. How two visionaries ignited the Dallas
Ballroom scene." dallasvoice.com/walk-burn-pose

"Women in Drag," *Curve* magazine.

Research sources

Boyce and terrorist drag: www.nytimes.com/2019/06/16/us/revisiting-stonewall-memories-history.html

Divine: www.them.us/story/drag-herstory-divine

First drag queen: newhistories.group.shef.ac.uk/the-trial-of-princess-seraphina-the-first-recognisable-drag-queen-in-english-history/

History of drag: https://www.npr.org/2019/06/27/736320026/how-drag-queens-have-sashayed-their-way-through-history

History of drag kings: blog.britishnewspaperarchive.co.uk/2021/03/11/vesta-tilley-male-impersonators/

Three articles of clothing rule: www.history.com/news/stonewall-riots-lgbtq-drag-three-article-rule

William Dorsey Swann: www.pinknews.co.uk/2020/10/13/first-drag-queen-slave-washington-dc-balls-emancipation-channing-gerard-joseph-william-dorsey-swann/

Index

Picture credits

Illustrations by Camila Gray. Backgrounds from Shutterstock/Hugo Lacasse & Alandesign. Other images from Alamy Stock Photo and: page 34 ZUMA Press, Inc.; 39 Pictorial Press Ltd.; 45 Richard Prudhomme; 53 Pacific Press Media Production Corp.; 67 Gianni Muratore; 70 agefotostock; 73 Adrian Sherratt; 75 Historic Collection; 77 Historic Images; 79 SBS Eclectic Images; 85 Photo 12; 90 ZUMA Press, Inc.; 105 David Grossman; 107 REUTERS; 111 United Archives GmbH.

Acknowledgments

Thank you to Dog 'n' Bone books for this amazing opportunity to share my love, heart, and knowledge of drag with the world. Thank you to Dana Barber for being there with me from the beginning of my solo drag and entrepreneur adventures. Your belief, support, and celebration of/with/in me is a big reason I finished and saw through every single project that led to this one. A special thank you to Sora Schilling, my mentor at the time of writing this book. Your reframes and encouragement completely shifted my mindset and, ultimately, the course of this book. Thank you to *mi familia* for your encouraging words, advice, support, and love. I have felt no greater royalty than being your child. Thank you to all the drag artists who have and continue to inspire me and the world with their art. Y'all are the *real* superstars of drag. Thank you to my wife who spent way too much time by herself while I was finishing up this book. I love you. This is only the beginning. We have so much further to journey together. *It is time*. And finally, a big thank you to my 20-year old self. Because without my own tenacity, courage, and conviction to prove the world and haters wrong, I never would have started my adventures in drag. And I never would have finished and self-published the book that landed me *this* gig.

Dream big, folxs. It happens when you least expect it.

BRANDI AMARA SKYY grew up under the south Texas sun, with rhinestone beaches, and full *familia* tamale-making kitchen table wisdom. As a double Leo (Rising + Moon), they have been everything performative under the sun: belly dancer, modern dancer, and award-winning drag queen. In their 20+ years in drag as a performer, pageant judge, and academic, Brandi has made history by winning the first Miss Diva USofA in 2014; creating the first haute drag magazine, *GAG Magazine*; and writing the first academic book fully focused on female drag queens, *Faux Queens—Fauxing the Real*, and the first all-gender-inclusive book on drag, *How to Be a Drag Queen: a guidebook for female drag queens and emerging drag artists*. Brandi is also the founder and Head Witch in Charge of WOKE MAGIC (www.wokemagic.com), an online bodega, publishing haus, a forthcoming Oracle Deck and Anthology, and a mentorship community for spirit-centered